BEWARE!

THIS SPOOKY BOOK BELONGS TO:

NAME:

∙∙

AGE:

∙∙

LET'S GET STARTED!

Here are some hints and tips for using scratch and draw paper to make cool decorations, drawings, and other ideas.

Use the sharpened stylus to draw on your scratch sheet to reveal the neon surface below.

Practice drawing simple shapes. Use thin lines for swirls or detail and thick lines for outlines.

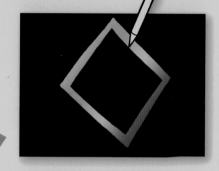

You can use tracing paper to transfer the outline of a picture onto scratch paper.

2 Put the tracing paper on top of the scratch paper and go over the lines.

3 You'll be able to see faint transfer lines, ready for scratching.

1 Draw a picture onto tracing paper in pencil.

USE THE STYLUS

This book comes with a wooden stylus. Sharpen one end with a pencil sharpener and use it like a pen or pencil on the scratch paper.

BE MEAN WITH THE PAPER!

Most of the project ideas in this book can be made any size you like. Before starting each project, think about the size you need and then cut the scratch paper to the size you want.

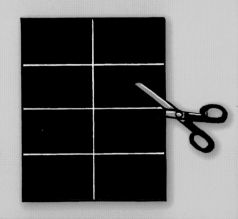

4

PROTECT YOUR WORK!

Scratch paper marks very easily, so it is a good idea to use a scrap of paper to hold the scratch paper while you're drawing.

MAKE MARKS!

Experiment with different implements to make marks on the scratch paper. For example, a fork works really well for making parallel lines.

TIP
Try making simple stencils to use on scratch paper.

SCRATCH AND SQUIGGLE

Make different sorts of marks according to the effect you want to achieve.

Repeat patterns to make interesting surfaces.

Use hatching to make an object look 3-D.

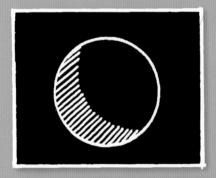

Cross-hatching is a good way to make an object look 3-D.

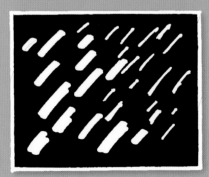

Make heavy or light marks with different tools or by using more or less pressure.

SPOOKY LETTERING

Draw your own spooky alphabet. Copy the style of the letters below and write your own spine-tingling words.

ABCDE

FGHIJK

LMNOP

QRSTU

VWXYZ

JACK-O'-LANTERN

Make a scary pumpkin that will petrify people.
Use a scratch paper and thin, colored card.

1 Draw the outline of a pumpkin shape on a scratch sheet. Add a stalk to the top.

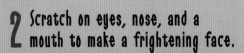

2 Scratch on eyes, nose, and a mouth to make a frightening face.

3 Use scissors to cut out the head.

4 Fold two small pieces of thin colored card into "V" shapes. Cut a small slot at the top of both pieces of card.

5 Slide the pumpkin head into the two slots so it stands up.

SCARY SKELETON

Draw a glowing skeleton skull that will chill you to the bone! Beware!

1 Copy this skeleton skull onto a colored scratch sheet.

2 Place a coin around the outline of your drawing. Scratch thin lines outward and away from the coin to create a glowing effect!

SPOOKY SPIDER

Draw an itsy-bitsy spider dangling from its web.
This looks cool on a white scratch sheet.

1 Draw a continuous spiral. Leave some space in one of the bottom corners.

2 Add diagonal lines coming out from the center.

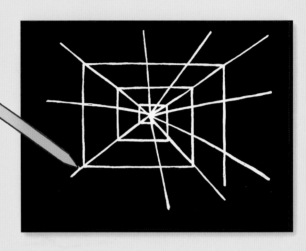

3 Draw the outline of a spider hanging from a piece of silky thread.

4 Add scary-looking details to the spider's face.

TIP
Put your creepy crawler in a dark corner to scare your friends.

HAUNTED HOUSE

Draw an eerie scene of a haunted house.
Then make a frame to show off your spooky art.

1 Draw a jagged line along the bottom as grass. Add angular trees without any leaves. Put in some tombstones.

2 Draw a haunted house with lots of roofs, towers, and arched windows, with pointed tops. This style is called "gothic."

3 Glue your picture to a piece of colored card. Cut a fancy shape around it to make a frame.

GLUE

GHOULISH GRAVEYARD

Make a spooky graveyard scene with terrifying tombstones!

1 Mark a line about 0.5" (10 mm) from the bottom of a scratch sheet.

2 Draw a tombstone shape on the scratch sheet. Add a design such as a skull and crossbones.

3 Cut out the top section of the tombstone. Fold the bottom edge and stand it up.

4 Make other tombstone shapes to create a mini graveyard.

BOO!

Shock your friends by making them a cool card with a spooky surprise inside.

1 Fold a piece of colored card in half. Cut two lines, as shown.

2 Open the card and bend the center part in, as shown.

3 Draw a ghost and a speech bubble with the word "Boo!" inside. Cut the ghost out.

4 Glue the ghost to the pop-up part. Add a scary sketch to the background.

GLUE

CRAZY CAT

Make a crazy-looking cat that will give you goosebumps in the night!

1 Fold a piece of scratch paper in half.

2 On both sides, draw a hair-raising cat with an arched back.

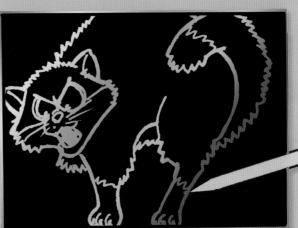

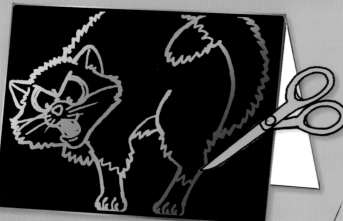

3 Cut out the cat, but don't cut along his back, or the card won't stay joined together.

4 Stand the cat up on a flat surface. Shine a flashlight at it and a spooky shadow will appear.

SCREAM!

This spine-tingling picture is perfect for a Halloween card.

1 Draw a ghostly skull and haunted house. It will look spookier if you draw at an angle.

2 Add hills, bats, a path, and a crescent moon.

3 Fold a piece of thin, colored card, about 10" x 8" (250 mm x 200 mm), in half. Glue your picture to the front.

4 Open the card and write your mysterious message inside.

CREEPY CASTLE

Make a spooky stencil by creating a creepy silhouette of a castle.

1 On a piece of thin card the same size as one of the white scratch sheets, draw the outline of a castle on a hill.

2 Cut out the design to make a stencil.

3 Hold the stencil in place and scratch away the background.

4 Remove the stencil and an outline of a creepy castle is left in black.

PUMPKIN PATCH

Scare your neighbors with some pumpkin window decorations.

1 Draw as many pumpkins as you can fit on one scratch sheet.

2 Cut out the pumpkin heads and tape them to a piece of string. Decorate your window.

TIP
Find inspiration on the other pages and create different spooky window decorations.

BATTY BOOKMARK

Make a blood-curdling bookmark to keep guard over your pages.

1 Cut a piece of scratch paper in half, lengthways.

2 Draw a long, thin bat with a scary face.

3 Cover the bookmark with a self-adhesive laminating sheet.

4 Cut out the bat shape using scissors.

MORE IDEAS
Here are some more great bookmark shapes to make:

Ghost

Tombstone

Witch's hat

WOBBLY WITCH'S HAT

Create a wicked wobbling decoration to hang from shelves and spook anyone who sees it.

1 Find some thin, transparent plastic packaging (such as the lids of takeout food containers). Cut strips about 0.5" x 4" (15 mm x 100 mm).

2 Draw a witch's hat on a section of a scratch paper.

3 Cut out the shape and tape it to a length of plastic. Fix the other end to a shelf with sticky tack or double-sided tape.

4 Make other decorations with the leftover scratch paper, such as a ghost, pumpkin, or witch's cat.

MYSTERY TRAIN

Make a creepy pencil topper, such as this ghost train.
It will give anyone the heebie-jeebies!

1 Cut a piece of scratch paper and fold it in half.

2 Draw a ghoulish ghost train on the front and back. Make sure it has a chimney with smoke. Cut out.

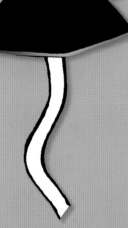

3 Glue the two halves together, with a twist tie or a pipe cleaner between the two halves.

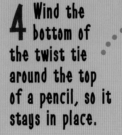

4 Wind the bottom of the twist tie around the top of a pencil, so it stays in place.

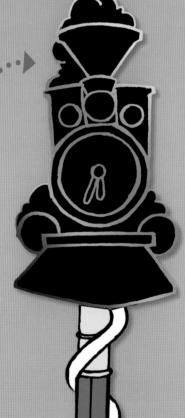

TIP
Try these spooky designs, too.

19

VAKEY VAKEY!

It's time to wake up your creepy friend—if you're brave enough!

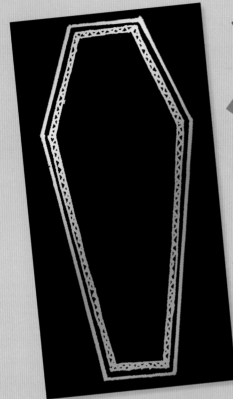

1 Scratch the outline of a coffin onto two scratch sheets.

TIP
Experiment with the colors revealed by your scratching. The shimmering, changing shades can look very creepy indeed!

2 On the top sheet, decorate it like a coffin lid. Use your imagination—draw designs you have seen on tombstones or spooky films.

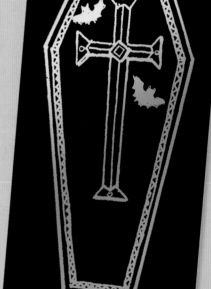

3 Scratch a vampire onto the other coffin shape. Cut out both shapes.

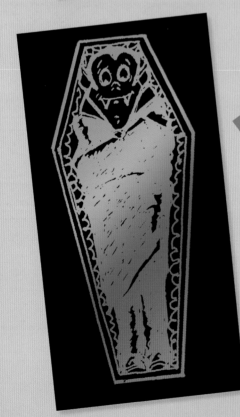

4 Tape the two coffin shapes together along one side to make a lid.

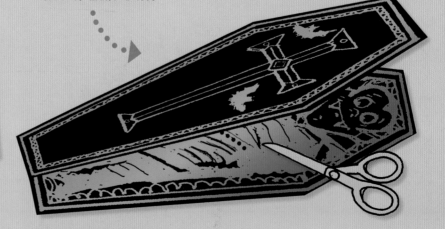

EYE CAN SEE YOU!

Use white or colored scratch sheets to make a greeting card.

1 Decide on the shape you want your card to be— a tombstone, a coffin or a simple rectangle?

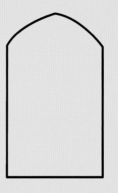
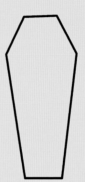
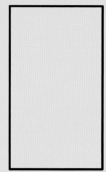

2 Fold the scratch sheet in two and cut out your shape. Decorate the front.

TIP
Practice drawing scary eyes onto scrap paper first.

Boo!

Happy Halloween

3 Really go to town with lots of eyes staring out at you. Creepy!

Happy Halloween

4 Add your Halloween message inside.

HEY, SUCKERS!

Make these cool straws for spooky parties.

1 Choose your favorite outline and copy it onto a piece of scratch paper. Cut it out.

2 Make a front and back side by copying the same outline onto another scratch sheet. Cut them out and decorate them.

3 Cut a hole where the mouth will be and decorate the face.

 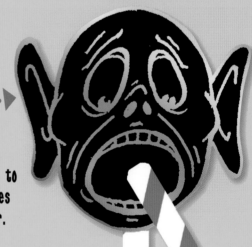

3 Use a dab of glue to stick the two sides of the head together.

22

SCAREDY CAT

There must be something REALLY sinister happening if a witch's cat is scared!

1 Copy this outline of a cat. Follow the instructions on page 4 if you want to trace it.

2 Add details—as much or as little as you like. Try eyes and whiskers, or lots of spiked fur standing up along its back.

3 Draw a narrow rectangle below the feet, as shown.

4 Cut around the whole shape and bend back the rectangle so the cat stands up.

TIP
Use ordinary black construction paper to make silhouettes of a witch and a cauldron for a whole spooky scene.

MAKE YOUR OWN SCRATCH & DRAW PAPER

You can make your own scratch paper.
You need thick paper or cardboard, and crayons or water-based paint.

1 Cover a piece of paper or card with the background color or colors of your choice.

2 Completely cover the background with black crayon.

3 You can also use paint to cover the background, though some paint is harder to scratch when dry—experiment first!

4 Use your homemade scratch paper to create new designs. You could also add a scent by dripping a couple drops of a favorite scent onto the paper.